THIS CANDLEWICK BOOK BELONGS TO:

_____

_____

_____

_____

For my dearest Rikka

First U.S. paperback edition 1994
First published in Great Britain in 1992 by Walker Books Ltd., London.

The Library of Congress has cataloged the hardcover edition as follows:

Alborough, Jez.
Where's my teddy? / Jez Alborough.
Summary: When a small boy named Eddie goes searching
for his lost teddy in the dark woods, he comes across a gigantic
bear with a similar problem.
ISBN 978-1-56402-048-2 (hardcover)
[1. Teddy bears—Fiction. 2. Bears—Fiction.
3. Stories in rhyme.] I. Title.
PZ8.3.A24Wh 1992
[E]—dc20   91-58765

ISBN 978-1-56402-280-6 (paperback)

14 15 16 17 18 19 SWT 36 35 34 33 32 31

Printed in Dongguan, Guangdong, China

This book was typeset in Garamond.
The illustrations were done in watercolor, crayon, and pencil.

Candlewick Press
99 Dover Street
Somerville, Massachusetts 02144

visit us at www.candlewick.com

WHERE'S MY TEDDY?

by Jez Alborough

CANDLEWICK PRESS

Eddie's off to find his teddy.
Eddie's teddy's name is Freddie.

He lost him in the woods somewhere.
It's dark and horrible in there.

"Help!" said Eddie. "I'm scared already!
I want my bed! I want my teddy!"

He tiptoed
on and on
until . . .

something
made him stop
quite still.

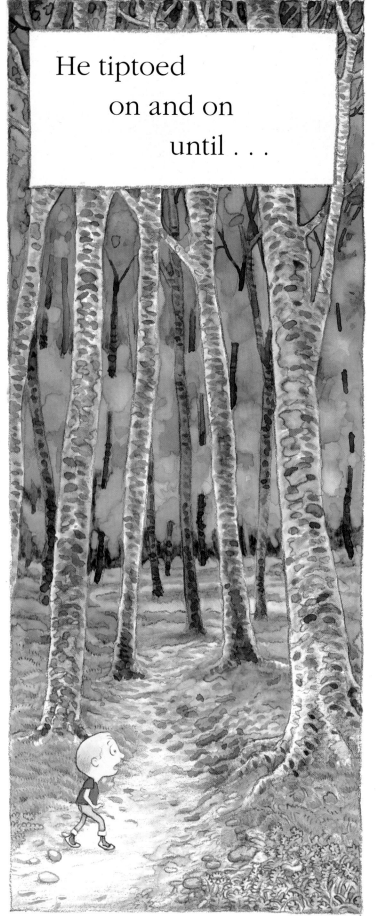

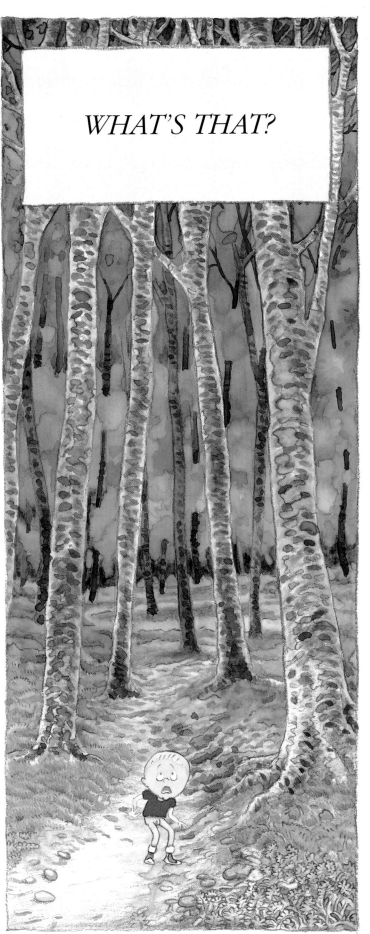

A GIANT TEDDY BEAR!
"Is it Freddie?" said Eddie.
"What a surprise!
How *did* you get to be this size?"

"You're too big to huddle and cuddle," he said,

"and I'll never fit both of us into my bed."

Then out of the darkness,
clearer and clearer,
the sound of sobbing
came nearer and nearer.

Soon the whole woods
could hear the voice bawl,
"How did you get to be
tiny and small?
You're too small to
huddle and cuddle," it said,
"and you'll only get lost
in my giant-sized bed!"

It was a gigantic bear
and a tiny teddy
stomping toward . . .

the giant teddy and Eddie.

"MY TED!"
gasped the bear.
"A BEAR!"
screamed Eddie.

"A BOY!"
yelled the bear.
"MY TEDDY!"
cried Eddie.

Then they ran and they ran
through the dark woods
back to their homes
as fast as they could . . .

all the way back
to their snuggly beds,
where they huddled
and cuddled their
own little teds.